SECRETS IN THE ATTIC

**Other Apple® paperbacks
you will enjoy:**

Ghosts Beneath Our Feet
    by Betty Ren Wright
The Dollhouse Murders
    by Betty Ren Wright
Who's Reading Darci's Diary?
    by Martha Tolles
The Computer That Said Steal Me
    by Elizabeth Levy

SECRETS IN THE ATTIC

Carol Beach York

AN
APPLE®
PAPERBACK

SCHOLASTIC INC.
New York Toronto London Auckland Sydney

ISBN 0-590-40607-8

12 11 10 9 8 7 6 5 4 3 2   7 8 9/8 0 1/9

Printed in the U.S.A.   11

SECRETS IN THE ATTIC

Prologue

Jodie would never forget that time last March when they had to say good-bye to Aunt Winifred. It had been cold, windy, and gray all day, echoing Jodie's own sadness. All around, outside Aunt Winifred's house, a chill and gloomy afternoon covered the woods and countryside.

Inside the house, lamps were lit. Jodie was sent into the hall to watch her little brother, Peter, while her mother and Great Aunt Winifred talked. The two women sat opposite one another in Aunt Winifred's beautiful living room, where a bright fire burned in the fireplace and a large brass peacock stood guard beside the hearth.

"Stay with Peter for a few minutes," her mother had said, touching Jodie's shining black hair and turning her gently away from the living room. "I want to talk to Aunt Winifred."

Peter, just three years old, was sitting on the bottom step of the curving hall stairway. The large

1

hall was a good place to play, and he was waiting patiently for Jodie to join him.

She knew what her mother was going to talk to Aunt Winifred about: Mama and Jodie and Peter were going to move away from their house in East Hill. They were going to move away from the only house Jodie had ever lived in, from the only place she had ever known. It made Jodie want to cry. But crying wouldn't help, all the plans were made. Now Mama was going to tell Aunt Winifred, and Jodie had to keep Peter busy so Mama and Aunt Winifred could talk.

As she passed the living room doorway, playing with Peter, Jodie could hear their voices and make out a word now and then ". . . happier in a new town," Mama was saying, ". . . away from the gossip, and from people like Claire."

While they talked, Mama and Aunt Winifred were drinking tea. Jodie could see the firelight dancing on the teacups, and the glow of the lamps reflected in the large windows of the living room. Whenever she had a chance, she peeked anxiously into the room. How pretty her mother looked in her dark green silk dress, with her chestnut hair curling around her face. Aunt Winifred's white hair was set off by the soft blue of her dress.

"Come here, Jodie." Aunt Winifred smiled at Jodie and beckoned. "Come here, darling."

Jodie hurried into the living room, across the

flowered carpeting. Peter held on to her hand tightly.

"Who's this?" Mama said, and Peter threw himself into her lap, shouting, "Pete!"

The flames flickered in the grate. Beyond the windows, where the draperies had not yet been drawn, Jodie could see the woods, and the trees standing stiffly in the fading afternoon light.

Aunt Winifred leaned toward Mama's chair and patted Peter's arm. "Jodie will find something for you to play with," she said. Her kindly face was lined with the smiles and worries of eighty years. The hand she reached toward Peter was thin and blue-veined, and trembled slightly. "Jodie will go up to the attic and find something nice for you to play with."

The attic was cold and shadowy. Jodie switched on the overhead light that lit the front section, where the toys were kept. What could she find for Peter?

She stood looking at the toy shelves, remembering the many times she had played here in Aunt Winifred's attic, wondering when she would play here again. I hope we'll come back sometimes, Jodie thought. She didn't want to think that maybe they would never visit Aunt Winifred again.

Jodie stood staring at the two shelves of toys, feeling miserable, and worrying about moving to a new town and going to a new school. At last she shook herself back to the present and studied the toys. She chose a toy monkey from the top shelf. It was soft and fluffy, with black glass eyes. It was only a little worn from being played with over the years.

Her glance lingered along the shelves of toys. She wanted to remember all of them, the ones she had played with, the ones her father and uncle had said they played with when they were little boys. The toys were reminders of good times past.

Finally she turned off the attic light and went downstairs, where the firelight flickered on the brass peacock and the silver tea tray.

Upstairs in the attic, darkness settled around the old toys.

One

It was almost Christmas. There were only three more days of school before Christmas vacation.

Jodie and her best friend Doreen had stayed after school to help their teacher, Miss Nelson, put up a display of science papers on the bulletin board at the back of Room 204. All the other children had gone.

"Thanks a lot, girls," Miss Nelson said, sending them off at last with a wave and a smile. The corridor was deserted, silent. Jodie and Doreen snatched their coats and caps from the locker they shared, and clattered down the stairs and out through the main door of Whittier School.

Doreen's plump face quickly got red from the cold and the exertion of running to keep up with Jodie as they raced home, leaving behind the school where every room had a paper wreath or a Santa Claus or snowflakes in its windows. A tall fir tree with only one flat side stood by the stage in the gym, where the Christmas program would be held on the last day of school.

The girls finally slowed down to a walk, after Jodie slipped and fell down on some snowy patches, and Doreen was panting and out of breath.

"You're lucky to be going away for Christmas," Jodie said, brushing snow from the side of her coat. Doreen's whole family was going to her uncle's farm for Christmas. It seemed to Jodie that Doreen had all the fun. She had to wear braces to straighten her teeth, but that wasn't so bad, when everything else in Doreen's life was just about perfect, as far as Jodie could see.

"I can hardly wait," Doreen said eagerly. "My grandparents will be there, too."

"That sounds like so much fun," Jodie said longingly. "We used to have big Christmases like that when we lived in East Hill and my daddy was alive."

"I know," Doreen said comfortingly. She knew Jodie's father had died in an automobile accident, and thought that was the saddest thing she could think of. She slipped her arm through Jodie's and gave it a little comforting squeeze.

"My Aunt Winifred has a big house, and we always had Christmas dinner there. My Uncle Phillip and Aunt Claire always came, and my cousin Lisa. Lisa sort of bugs me sometimes, she thinks she's so perfect. . . ." Jodie's voice trailed off. Ahead she could see some boys playing in the yard at Tommy Henley's house. Doreen had a crush on Tommy Henley, and Jodie gave her a nudge, in case she hadn't noticed that Tommy was out in his yard.

Doreen had noticed. Her face got even pinker. She put her lips together tight so her braces wouldn't show. Then as they drew near the house she looked the other way, so the boys would think she wasn't interested, especially Tommy. Doreen didn't want him to know she liked him.

"Is he looking, is he looking?" she asked, without moving her lips.

"Sure he's looking — " Jodie started to say, but the boys were doing more than that. They had come to the edge of the yard. "Hey Jodie — hey, Doreen!" they shouted. When the girls looked around, snowballs came whizzing over the fence and they had to run for cover.

"You're *terrible!*" Doreen turned back from a safe distance and stuck her tongue at Tommy and his friends. Then she put her arm through Jodie's again and they went on, heads together, whispering and giggling about the boys.

When they reached Jodie's house Doreen came in to have cocoa. Sometimes after school they went to Doreen's house and made fudge; sometimes they went to the library together. If Doreen had to go

7

to the dentist to get her braces tightened after school, Jodie just came home by herself.

Jodie looked in the porch mailbox before they went into the house. If the mailman was late, the mail would still be in the box when she came home from school.

There was mail in the box now, a lot of it; mostly envelopes with Christmas stamps that Jodie knew were Christmas cards. The mail was always exciting at Christmastime. The envelope on the very top of the pile was from Aunt Winifred — Jodie spotted her name right away: Winifred Sutton.

The moment she saw the address Jodie was overwhelmed with longing. She wished they were going to East Hill for Christmas — to Aunt Winifred's beautiful house, where they'd had so many happy times — where they never went anymore.

But Jodie didn't say anything. Doreen was stamping snow from her boots. Jodie's little brother Peter, who had been at the window watching for them, already had the front door open. Jodie gathered up the few other pieces of mail that were at the back of the box, and added them carefully to the stack of envelopes.

Once inside the house Doreen tugged off her boots and put her coat over the post at the end of the stairs. Jodie kicked off her boots and left them on the mat at the side of the door.

The house wasn't as big as the one they had had in East Hill, but it was a pretty little house. The dining room windowsills were lined with plants, and there was a beautiful old grandfather clock on the landing of the stairway. There was a fat green tree in the living room, shining with ornaments and strands of silvery icicles.

Jodie was still wearing her coat and cap as she and Doreen went through the hallway to the kitchen, where her mother was making the cocoa.

"Look, Mama, here's a letter from Aunt Winifred — we haven't had a letter from her in a long time." Jodie put the rest of the mail on the kitchen table and held up the envelope with Aunt Winifred's address in the corner.

Jodie's mother glanced at the envelope casually. "It's probably a Christmas card," she said.

"Can I open it?"

"Yes, go ahead." Mama was putting miniature marshmallows in the bottoms of three cups. Peter was eating the marshmallows out of his cup as fast as she put them in. When the cocoa was hot, Mama would pour it over the marshmallows and they would bob to the top like little white buttons and then melt into a wonderful gooey layer over the top of the cocoa.

"Just a couple more, and that's absolutely all," Mama said, as she put three more tiny marshmallows into Peter's cup.

Jodie slit open Aunt Winifred's envelope, and it wasn't a Christmas card at all. It was a letter. The stationery was pale blue, Aunt Winifred's favorite color, and the edges were soft and lacy, not sharp and straight like most paper edges were.

"It's not a Christmas card," Jodie said. "It's a real letter, see?" Maybe Aunt Winifred was writing to invite them to come for Christmas! Wouldn't that be great!

Jodie's mother poured the cocoa into the cups and looked at the letter Jodie held out to her. She didn't seem to be as happy as Jodie was to be getting a letter from Aunt Winifred. "I wonder why she's writing?" she murmured to herself.

Doreen sat down at the kitchen table and tasted her cocoa. It was too hot to drink. She took the spoon out of the saucer and pushed the marshmallows around, watching them melt.

"Is that your aunt who lives in the big house, where you used to go every Christmas?" Doreen looked up at Jodie and then at Jodie's mother. There was a tension she didn't understand. Why wasn't Jodie's mother as excited about the letter as Jodie was? What was wrong?

Jodie nodded at Doreen silently. She waited impatiently as her mother read the letter to herself. While she waited she took off her coat and hung it on the back of a kitchen chair. Finally she couldn't wait any longer.

"What does she say, Mama?"

"She wants us to come for Christmas."

"She does!" Jodie's wish had come true, only minutes after she wished it. Wouldn't it be wonderful if all the wishes came true that fast! Jodie felt like jumping up and down and hugging everybody.

" 'It will be a little family reunion,' " Mama was reading from the letter. " 'Claire and Lisa will come, too, so I hope you and Jodie and Peter can join us. Families shouldn't drift apart.' "

Mama was frowning as she finished the letter.

" 'Please come, so we can all spend Christmas together and things can be the way they used to be.' "

Jodie knew from the expression on Mama's face that they weren't going to Aunt Winifred's for Christmas, but she couldn't quite give up hope. "Doreen's going to her uncle's farm for Christmas," she said, pouring out the words. "Everybody will be there, like it used to be for us at Aunt Winifred's. Oh, Mama, couldn't we please go, *please?*"

Jodie's mother smiled gently. "You loved Christmas at Aunt Winifred's, didn't you?"

"Oh, yes!" Jodie said. "And I remember *everything!*"

Peter came to stand at the table to see if his cocoa was cool enough to drink. Jodie knew he probably didn't remember much about Aunt Winifred's house, he was so little. But Jodie remembered it all. Christmastime at Aunt Winifred's had always been so much fun. Logs burning in the big fireplace, Mrs. Crofton in the kitchen baking pies and stuffing the Christmas turkey, the snowy woods all around like a fairyland.

Aunt Winifred always had a big Christmas tree, trimmed with the special ornaments she had saved from her childhood, ornaments you couldn't buy in stores anymore. Everything was special about Christmas at Aunt Winifred's.

"I suppose you could go alone," Mama said, looking at Jodie's disappointed face. "Would you want to do that, honey?"

Jodie hesitated. Go alone? Go to Aunt Winifred's without Mama and Peter?

"Jodie?" Mama was waiting for an answer. Doreen was smiling.

Slowly Jodie shook her head. "I wouldn't want to be away from you and Peter on Christmas Day."

"We'd miss you, too," Mama said. "If you really want to go, how about the day after Christmas? You could stay the whole week between Christmas and New Year's. I'm sure Aunt Winifred would like that."

"That sounds great," Doreen said, and Jodie began to smile. "Okay," she said, "that's what I'll do. I'll go the day after Christmas."

Two

That night as Jodie was getting ready for bed she began to have second thoughts about visiting Aunt Winifred. Did she really want to go that far away by herself and be alone with Aunt Claire and Lisa for a whole week? If Mama and Peter were coming along, that would be different. But they weren't. Maybe it would be better if she just forgot the whole thing and stayed home.

She heard a soft rap at the edge of her open door.

"Hi, sweetie." Mama came in and sat on the side of Jodie's bed. She watched as Jodie brushed her shining, dark hair. "Aunt Winifred won't know you," she said. "You've grown so much this past year."

"Why don't you want to go, Mama?" Jodie lowered her arm, forgetting about her hair for the moment. "It would be so much more fun if you and Peter came along."

Jodie's mother shook her head. "I'm not ready to cope with your Aunt Claire."

"But *why*?" Jodie wanted to know. "What's so bad about Aunt Claire?"

Mama looked unhappy. She moved her finger back and forth across Jodie's bedspread, in an aimless zigzag pattern.

"You remember when Mr. Carrington's money was stolen . . . and no one knew who had stolen it?" Mama paused. "Aunt Claire said it was Daddy."

"Daddy?" Jodie felt her hands begin to tremble as she put down the hair brush. "Daddy wouldn't steal anything!"

"No, of course he wouldn't," Mama said quickly. "But the money was never found. And then Daddy had that car accident, so he could never defend himself against Aunt Claire's accusations."

"Why did Aunt Claire think Daddy took the money?"

"She wasn't the only one," Mama said. "Daddy was Mr. Carrington's attorney, and he had access to his safety deposit box. Usually Mr. Carrington didn't keep large sums of cash in the box." Jodie's mother lifted her hands in a helpless gesture. "This was for some special business deal he was involved in. If he hadn't had a heart attack and died so suddenly, the theft wouldn't have been discovered so quickly. It was a shock to everybody."

"And Aunt Claire said Daddy took it?" Jodie

could feel herself beginning to get angry. She began to brush her hair furiously. How dare Aunt Claire think such a thing. How dare she! And Aunt Claire would be at Aunt Winifred's house for Christmas, sipping her coffee at dinner and smiling across the table at Aunt Winifred: Of course Charles took the money, it's obvious, anyone can see. . . . Jodie should be there to defend her father, maybe somehow she could even prove that he was innocent. Here is the real thief, Aunt Claire!

Visions whirled in Jodie's mind.

"Jodie?" Mama was trying to get her attention. "You've brushed that section of hair a dozen times. What are you thinking?"

Jodie held the brush in her lap. "If I go to Aunt Winifred's, maybe I can help somehow."

Jodie's mother got up from the edge of the bed. "I don't know what you could do to help, honey. But I hope you have a happy time at Aunt Winifred's."

"Did Uncle Phillip think Daddy took the money?"

Mama shook her head. "No, he didn't. He was pretty upset about it, of course, because he was a vice-president of the bank where Mr. Carrington had his safety deposit box. It was bad publicity for the bank. He said we'd find out the truth. But then he died, too, before he had a chance to do anything."

Jodie nodded sadly. Uncle Phillip had been in

the car with Daddy when it skidded on the snowy road. Uncle Phillip was dead, too; he couldn't help find the real thief.

"But wasn't there anybody else?" Jodie insisted. "Wasn't there anybody else who could have stolen the money?"

"Well," Mama said thoughtfully, "Mr. Carrington did have a nephew who was rumored to be heavily in debt. Some people thought he had stolen the money, but there was no proof."

"There was no proof against Daddy, was there?" Jodie asked with alarm. Mama shook her head firmly. "Not a bit, honey. But he was Mr. Carrington's attorney and he had a key to the safe deposit box. Some people thought that was proof enough. Aunt Claire for one. But that's enough talk for tonight — you've got school tomorrow."

Mama went toward the door, smiling back at Jodie.

"It will be your first time on a train by yourself," she reminded Jodie.

"I'll be okay," Jodie promised. "I'll be just fine."

Three

Christmas day was cold and dark. Skimpy, hard-driven little flakes of snow whirled past the windows as Jodie and Peter looked out.

The living room behind them was strewn with toys, and boxes and ribbons from the Christmas gifts. Dinner was cooking in the kitchen and the whole house smelled marvelous. If only Daddy could be with them, Jodie thought, everything would be perfect. Probably everything *was* perfect for Peter, because he was too little to remember Daddy the way she and Mama did. And he didn't know anything about Mr. Carrington's money, of course.

The money was like a secret, Jodie thought, a secret no one knew except the person who had stolen it.

Finding out this secret wouldn't bring Daddy back, but Jodie had to prove that her father was not a thief, like Aunt Claire and a lot of other people thought. But how could she do it? Perhaps

17

Mr. Carrington's relatives had found the money. What if it had only been misplaced, and not stolen by anyone? Jodie thought.

Maybe she would find a note her father had written saying that he knew who had stolen the money. She would find the note in an old book, or at the back of a drawer no one used much . . . some place like that.

Or maybe somebody — the real thief — would come forward and confess and return all of the money.

Oh, I'm so sorry I ever thought your father was a thief, Aunt Claire would say. I was so unkind. Can you ever forgive me?

Jodie realized how foolish these daydreams were. If anyone had found the money, Mama would know. Aunt Winifred would have written.

Jodie watched the snowflakes spin by the window in the cold wind. Moving to Whittier hadn't been as bad as she had expected. She had Doreen for a best friend, and she liked Whittier School. The Christmas program had been terrific on the last day of school.

Now Christmas vacation lay ahead . . . and the trip to Aunt Winifred's. What would it be like at Aunt Winifred's house? Again Jodie felt a pang of doubt. What was she getting into?

Peter had watched the snow long enough and was dragging a box from under the Christmas tree out into the middle of the living room floor. He pulled off the cardboard lid and dumped the contents onto the carpet. The pieces made clinking sounds as they jumbled together into a pile.

"Let's fix this," he called to Jodie, as Mama came from the kitchen, wearing her special red Christmas apron.

"That's nice," she said, sitting down in a chair by the Christmas tree. "You're putting the space station together."

"This is my best thing," Peter said happily.

"Is that so?" Mama laughed.

"What's your best thing, Jodie?" Peter looked up at Jodie solemnly.

"Oh, let me see. . . ." Jodie moved over toward the tree where she had piled her presents after she opened them. A new pair of boots — a shoulder-strap bag — a warm robe — a box of candy.

Memories of other Christmases flooded back. Ice skates when she was nine, a play stove. Little House books. And far, far back among the memories was the little yarn doll.

"Mama, do you still have my little yarn doll?" She looked at Mama in her chair by the side of the tree.

"Of course I do." Mama shook her head to think Jodie could ask such a question.

"You brought it along when we moved here?"

"Of course I did," Mama said. "I could never

19

throw that away. It was your favorite toy when you were little."

Jodie knew mothers saved things — baby booties, report cards, homemade Valentines, *and* favorite toys. It made Jodie happy to know that Mama had saved the little yarn doll all these years.

Jodie went to bed that night, happy about her Christmas day. But her trip to Aunt Winifred's tomorrow was even more on her mind. She wondered if everything was the same in East Hill. She was beginning to forget some things about East Hill after nearly a year, but other things she still remembered very clearly.

Mrs. Scott, the fifth-grade teacher who was more beautiful than a movie star. A church with tall stained-glass windows, that stood near the school. The swimming pool in the park, where she had learned to swim when she was six years old. Jodie remembered these things clearly.

And Mr. Carrington's house by the park. She remembered that, too. It was the biggest house in East Hill. Mr. Carrington had been very rich and very important.

Jodie wondered who lived in the house now that Mr. Carrington was dead. She had visited there once with her father, and remembered the wide stone steps leading up to the front door. Inside, the house had been very quiet and very big, and sort of scary.

Jodie thought about the house as she tried to get to sleep. Mr. Carrington had had a big green parrot in a cage in his living room. It was a huge cage. Jodie had never known anyone who had a real live parrot for a pet. Her friends had dogs or kittens. The boy next door had goldfish because his mother was allergic to dog and cat hair. But nobody had a parrot.

"Does your parrot talk?" Jodie had asked Mr. Carrington.

Mr. Carrington was a tall man with silvery-white hair and a small white mustache. He sat in a chair with his fingertips together like a steeple.

"No, it doesn't talk much," Mr. Carrington had said.

Jodie was disappointed.

Then Mr. Carrington told her not to put her fingers through the bars of the cage, because the parrot was not very friendly and sometimes nipped fingers when it was cross.

Jodie had been glad to get away from Mr. Carrington's big, silent, scary house and his big, silent, scary parrot.

As she grew sleepy her thoughts got all mixed up with Mr. Carrington's parrot and her visit to Aunt Winifred's and the Christmas Day just past.

Mama had saved her little yarn doll . . . all these years. . . .

Jodie was finally fast asleep. In her dream she was playing with her yarn doll. It was made of bright-colored yarn, with floppy arms and legs. Then the dream changed and Jodie was on a stairway, a stairway in Aunt Winifred's house. It was the stairway to the attic, where the toys were. Jodie held on tight to the little yarn doll, because the stairway was so dark. In her dream she felt surrounded by darkness, by secrets and favorite toys, and mysteries she didn't understand.

Four

It would take five hours to get to East Hill so Jodie had brought a lunch to eat on the train.

She had a turkey sandwich, a banana, and Christmas cookies. It was strange eating lunch on a train while the world went flying by the window — woods and fields white with snow, children sledding on a hillside, wintry scenes that sometimes made her sad as they flew by and vanished behind her. Daddy and Uncle Phillip had died in the wintertime, when Daddy's car skidded on a snowy road. Maybe if it hadn't been winter, they would still be alive.

Jodie pressed her cheek against the train window and watched the white fields and woods, cars on country roads, farm houses outlined against the sky. Doreen was at her uncle's farm house somewhere, Jodie thought. She would tell Jodie all about it when she came home, and Jodie would tell Doreen all about her visit to Aunt Winifred's.

As the train was pulling into a station, the woman

sitting next to Jodie re-arranged herself, and took up the handle of the purse that had been resting in her lap.

"My stop," she said, smiling at Jodie as she stood up. "I hope you have a nice visit at your aunt's."

They had talked together when the woman first came on the train, and Jodie had told her about going to visit Aunt Winifred.

"I'm going to visit my sister," the woman had said. "She has nine children."

"Nine children?" Jodie was amazed.

"Yes, indeed," the woman said. Then she smiled at Jodie. "It's a rather lively house."

The station where the woman got off was bustling with people. But after a moment Jodie could see the woman's red hat, and the woman saw Jodie. She waved good-bye one more time, and then disappeared into the station house as the train started to move.

Jodie had saved her banana from lunch, and ate it now. She thought about seeing her cousin. Lisa was older than Jodie by three years, and was already in high school. She was very pretty and all her clothes were pretty. She had blue eyes and curly golden hair. Not only that, she was talented, too. She played the piano. She had told Jodie that when she grew up she was going to go all over the world giving concerts and become famous.

Jodie ate her banana slowly and watched the scenery. The conductor came along just as she was finishing. "About another hour, young lady," he said, nodding at her to show he hadn't forgotten she wanted to get off at East Hill.

Jodie put the banana peel in the bag with her other lunch wrappers. There was nothing left to eat. Not even a cookie.

She hadn't seen Lisa since she moved to Whittier. Jodie squinted out at the sunlight sparkling across the snow. A lot could have happened since she saw Lisa last. Maybe she had freckles and straight hair by now.

But no — there was Lisa, standing by Aunt Winifred's car at the end of the train station — as pretty as ever. She had on a blue coat, and a blue-knit cap and scarf. Her curly yellow hair was shining in the sun. Jodie saw her right away as she stepped down from the train.

"Here you go, sweetheart." The conductor swung down from the train and set Jodie's suitcase on the ground. Lisa waved to Jodie then, but didn't come running over to hug her as Doreen would have done.

Suddenly Jodie felt homesick. Everything was strange. Her suitcase sitting on the platform beside her didn't even look like her own. She was all alone, a long way from home.

Aunt Winifred's chauffeur was standing beside the car with Lisa. Before Jodie had a chance to get too homesick he came striding across the red brick paving by the train tracks, welcoming Jodie with a broad smile on his ruddy face.

Jodie felt better at once. Crofton was here, and Mrs. Crofton must be at the house, cooking delicious things in the kitchen. She would be happy to see Jodie, who didn't feel so homesick or alone, thinking of that.

"Well, well, look at you," Crofton said, in a voice that was like a good warm hug.

As he picked up Jodie's suitcase, the conductor called, "Good-bye, young lady" and stepped back aboard the train. He tipped his hat to Jodie as the train started to move again.

Jodie waved back at him, and then walked with Crofton to Aunt Winifred's car.

"Your train was late," Lisa said. "I was freezing waiting here."

Then why didn't you wait in the car, Jodie thought. Lisa was bugging her already, and the visit had hardly started!

Crofton opened the door for Lisa and Jodie to get into the backseat of the car. No one else had come to meet the train, but that didn't surprise Jodie. She knew the cold bothered Aunt Winifred, and a few years ago she had broken her hip. Now she didn't go out much in wintry weather. And of course, Aunt Claire wouldn't be interested in the arrival of an eleven-year-old niece at a small town train station.

Aunt Winifred's house was almost three miles out of town. The train station was at the edge of town, and Jodie saw only a few scattered houses before the car was moving away along a narrow, winding road through winter woods.

Jodie smoothed her coat and put her purse on her lap the way the woman on the train had done. She knew Lisa was looking at her carefully, looking especially at Jodie's new Christmas boots.

It was hard for Jodie to think of something to say, and then Lisa asked, "How was Christmas? What did you get?"

She was about to tell her what, but before she could begin Lisa said, "I got three new sweaters, and this hat and scarf set — and I got perfume and some new tapes — " Jodie listened as Lisa recited a long list of Christmas gifts. "Anyway, I'm glad you finally got here," Lisa said at last. "There's nothing to *do*, just by myself here. Aunt Winifred sleeps all the time," Lisa said impatiently. "She's getting so old." Lisa shook her head, to show that this was never going to happen to *her*.

"She's making a new will, you know." Lisa turned and looked at Jodie. "And I bet we're in it."

"Do you think so?" Jodie felt uncomfortable

talking about Aunt Winifred's will. It didn't seem right to talk about getting money; getting rich maybe, because someone died.

"She's got to leave her money to somebody," Lisa answered matter-of-factly.

Jodie glanced toward the front seat, but the window between them was closed. Crofton couldn't hear what they were saying.

"It's just a question of who gets the most," Lisa said with a sly little smile. She looked as though she knew who was getting the most, and it was going to be herself.

"Why does somebody have to get the most?" Jodie played with the strap of her purse — something the calm lady on the train had not done.

Lisa looked at Jodie with disgust. "Everybody knows *somebody* gets the most. There's always a favorite who gets it."

Through a break in the trees they could see Aunt Winifred's house ahead. The large gray stone house stood back from the road on a small rise of ground that had seemed like a high hill to Jodie when she was a little girl.

Crofton turned into the driveway that led up to the house. Snow was banked on either side of it, and as Jodie looked toward the house she could see snow on the windowsills and snow drifts in the corners of the windows. It was like a Christmas card picture.

She knew the inside of the house so well. The fireplace in the living room. The warm, bright kitchen where Mrs. Crofton worked. The upstairs bedrooms with windows overlooking the wide lawns. The narrow little stairway that led up to the attic. Jodie knew it all.

She imagined Aunt Winifred, sitting at the elegant little desk, in her bedroom, making a will, writing in shaky, old-fashioned letters: *I leave all my money to Lisa, my favorite grand-niece.*

Was Lisa old enough to be in a will? Jodie glanced at her cousin, who was just then putting her hand up to smooth her pretty yellow hair. Maybe you had to be grown-up to be in a will, Jodie thought.

If children couldn't be in wills, then Aunt Winifred would probably leave the money to Aunt Claire. And Aunt Claire, as Jodie's father had always said, really knew how to spend money!

Five

Aunt Claire greeted Jodie at the door, looking as if she still knew how to spend money as well as ever. Her hair had recently been done at the hairdresser's, and in her expensive silk blouse and tailored black velvet slacks she looked like a model from the pages of a fashion magazine. Her perfume was exotic and somewhat overwhelming.

Jodie felt the aura of beauty salons, fashion boutiques, and hundred-dollar-an-ounce perfume as Aunt Claire hovered over her briefly, and gave a quick peck into the air at the side of Jodie's cheek.

"Darling," Aunt Claire said. Then she drew back to look at Jodie and reassure herself that her own Lisa was still the prettier of the two girls.

Crofton set Jodie's suitcase down in the hallway. But Aunt Claire flourished her hand and six thin, gold bracelets flew about. "Take the suitcase upstairs, please," she directed Crofton. "Jodie will be using the room at the end of the hall."

As Crofton disappeared up the wide, curving

stairway, Aunt Claire took Jodie's arm and drew her toward the living room.

"I'm the official welcomer," she said in a chatty voice, as though this should be a special treat for Jodie.

"Where's Aunt Winifred?" Jodie admired Aunt Claire's clothes and jewelry, but was thinking she'd rather see Aunt Winifred.

"Auntie's resting," Aunt Claire said.

Lisa followed them into the living room, carefully unbuttoning her blue coat. At the far end of the room the late afternoon light glimmered on the dark mahogany of Aunt Winifred's piano. A lamp, already lit on a table by the fireplace, shined up on the portrait of Aunt Winifred that had hung in the same spot ever since Jodie could remember. It was a portrait of her as a young woman. She was holding a fan and smiling with a merry, almost flirtatious expression. On another wall was a portrait of Aunt Winifred's husband, who had died before Jodie was born.

In front of the windows stood a splendid Christmas tree, glittering with tinsel. Feathered ornamental birds perched in the branches. Elves and angels dangled from silken cords. Aunt Claire touched a light switch and the tree glowed and seemed to fill the room.

"I'm hungry," Lisa said. "Can't Jodie and I have something before dinner? It's hours away."

Jodie was grateful to Lisa for the first time that day. It was a long time since she had eaten lunch on the train.

"It is *not* hours away," Aunt Claire replied airily, "but go along if you like. Mrs. Crofton will want to see Jodie anyway."

The girls put their coats away and hurried through the front hall to the dining room and on past the butler's pantry into the kitchen.

It was a large kitchen, with a center work counter and two built-in ovens. All of Mrs. Crofton's shiny, copper-bottomed pots and pans hung from hooks along the wall. Bowls and spoons cluttered the center counter, and the overhead fixture shed bright beams of light down on all the bowls, and on Mrs. Crofton's plump pink face. She was smiling with pleasure to see Jodie, and put down her big cooking spoon.

"You've grown so, I hardly know you," she said, hugging Jodie.

"Oh, you know me," Jodie said. She felt shy, although she had known Mrs. Crofton all her life.

Lisa went to the refrigerator and took out a package of cheese. She got a box of crackers from a cupboard, and a plate.

"We're having our hors d'oeuvres," she told Mrs. Crofton. Then she began to slice the cheese and arrange it on the crackers.

"I see you're as pretty as ever." The housekeeper waved toward a chair at the round kitchen table, and Jodie sat down. She still had on her boots, and noticed that Lisa had taken hers off somewhere along the way, and stood in her stocking feet arranging the cheese and crackers on the plate.

"And how's your pretty mother?" Mrs. Crofton asked. "And that cute little brother of yours? He's a big boy now, I expect."

"Peter goes to nursery school," Jodie said. "And Mama's fine. She could have come but. . . ." Her voice faded away. She had started to tell a lie, just to be polite. Mama had no intention of coming to Aunt Winifred's, and here she was making it sound like Mama really wanted to come.

Jodie was glad Mrs. Crofton had her mind on the dinner, and only half on what Jodie was saying.

"Pretty as a picture, your mother is," Mrs. Crofton declared. She swished her spoon in the bowl and added a few shakes of seasoning from the spice jars arranged on a tray at one end of the counter.

"And *your* mother, too." She wasn't going to leave Lisa out.

Lisa had begun to eat the crackers and she mumbled something that sounded like, "Tmmmm wumm."

Mrs. Crofton seemed to understand that. She was silent for a moment, rummaging among the spice jars for the exact one she wanted.

When Lisa had eaten most of the crackers and cheese, she brought the plate over to the table and let Jodie have the rest. She could have eaten a hundred, but there were only four left.

Fortunately, Jodie was able to find other things to eat while she waited for dinner. Aunt Winifred always had hard candies wrapped in bright-colored paper in a dish on the living room coffee table. Because it was Christmastime, there was a large, fancy, five-pound box of chocolates on the table, too. Christmas was the one time of year that there was plenty of candy around when you needed it, thought Jodie.

Mr. Anthony, Aunt Winifred's attorney, had been invited for dinner, and he sat in the leather wing chair by the fireplace. They were all waiting for Aunt Winifred to come downstairs.

While he talked with Aunt Claire, Jodie ate chocolates from the box on the coffee table, and then Lisa was persuaded to play a piece on the piano. "A little Chopin for Mr. Anthony," Aunt Claire suggested, glowing with pride.

Jodie sat on the floor by the Christmas tree, its red and green lights shining on her face, while Lisa played. Mr. Anthony sipped his sherry and nodded his head to show that he liked the piano playing.

"Ah, Chopin, Chopin," he kept repeating, although Aunt Claire frowned at him. She didn't like talking while Lisa played.

Mr. Anthony was almost as old as Aunt Winifred. He had been her lawyer for years, and Jodie wondered if he had come to talk about her new will. She wondered, too, if Mama was in the will. She looked at Mr. Anthony when he wasn't looking at her, but she couldn't get any clues from that, and nobody but Lisa had mentioned the word will.

Aunt Winifred came into the room just as the music was ending. Her white hair softly framed her face. The skin stretched across her cheeks looked as fragile as ancient paper. She moved more slowly than Jodie had remembered, and Aunt Claire jumped up when she saw her coming. "Here's Auntie now," she said.

Aunt Winifred held out her hand to Jodie.

"You've been away too long," she said gravely. "Let me look at you."

She looked at Jodie so lovingly and so intently that of course Mr. Anthony and Aunt Claire and Lisa looked at Jodie, too. She felt her face flushing from all the attention.

"How do you like your new home?" Aunt Winifred asked, patting Jodie's hand.

"It's nice," Jodie said. "I like it."

"And do you have some new friends there?"

"My best friend is Doreen."

"Ahhh." Aunt Winifred gave Jodie's hand an extra-special pat. "A best friend, that's very good, very good. And how is Peter?"

"He's fine."

Aunt Winifred's voice softened. "How is your dear mother? I did so wish she could be with us for the holidays."

"Mama's fine." Jodie didn't know what else to say. She couldn't say Mama didn't want to come because of Aunt Claire. Aunt Winifred nodded, looking Jodie straight in the eye. Jodie knew she understood why Mama didn't come.

"On to the feast," Aunt Winifred said abruptly, drawing Jodie along as she led the way to the dining room. There were four green candles in crystal candleholders lit on the table, and the food was delicious. Mrs. Crofton was a very good cook; Mr. Anthony said she cooked like an angel.

"I've had some superb food in my time," Mr. Anthony said, "but Mrs. Crofton's cooking wins the prize." He lifted his glass and proposed a toast to Mrs. Crofton.

When the glasses were lowered, Mr. Anthony looked around the table, toward Jodie and Lisa, and said, "Now what are you two young ladies going to be doing this week?"

The question seemed to hang in the air. Jodie glanced across the table at Lisa. Their eyes met.

They both knew it wasn't going to be like holidays of the past. Then, their fathers had been alive, and Jodie's mother and Peter had been there. Let's go skating out at the pond, Uncle Phillip would say, hearty and cheerful, making the whole day come alive. But Uncle Phillip was dead now. Come on, everybody, out to the car, Jodie's father would call, clapping his hands to get attention. We're going into town — come on, get your coats, get your boots — we're going to eat Chinese food to-night! It had always been fun and exciting. But Daddy and Uncle Phillip were gone now. . . .

"Lisa will be practicing her piano," Aunt Claire said lightly. "And there will be trips to town. There will be plenty to do."

Jodie was beginning to feel tired. It had been a long, eventful day.

The green candles burned lower.

Aunt Claire said something to Mr. Anthony and he answered gallantly, "You're much too young and pretty, Mrs. Linville, to stay alone very long. One of these days," he shook his finger at Aunt Claire playfully, "one of these days. Mark my words."

Lisa's face grew pale and anxious-looking. Tired as she was, Jodie could tell Lisa was upset by what Mr. Anthony had said.

Lisa didn't look at Jodie, or anyone else. She dropped her eyes and pushed the food around on her plate, pretending she hadn't heard what Mr. Anthony said.

Lisa feels just like I feel, when people tease Mama about getting married again, Jodie thought.

It was somehow a bond between Jodie and Lisa, that someday they might have new fathers. Except nobody could take Daddy's place, Jodie told herself with a surge of loyalty. She looked down at her plate for a moment. Someday it might happen. Maybe someday Mama *would* get married again.

Jodie felt tired and confused. As she looked up she saw Aunt Winifred smiling at her gently. She felt comforted, as though Aunt Winifred had patted her arm and said, "Don't worry, Jodie, things work out for the best."

Jodie smiled back at Aunt Winifred. She was happy to be visiting Aunt Winifred . . . even if everything else in her life wasn't perfect.

Six

There had been more snow during the night, and Crofton was clearing the driveway with a snowblower. While Lisa practiced the piano, Jodie watched Crofton from the living room window, and then decided to go outside herself.

As she sat on the bottom step of the hall stairs to put on her boots, she could still hear Lisa practicing in the living room. She was just getting warmed up now and the sound of the piano echoed through the rooms of the big, gray stone house. Even Mrs. Crofton way off in the kitchen could hear Lisa's piano practice.

Jodie closed the front door behind her and stood in the sudden silence of the white winter morning. She could see her breath in the clear, crisp air. Across the lawn a flurry of sparrows rising into the air loosened snow from the tree branch where they had been perched. Jodie watched the snow shed a fine, powdery trail as it fell. Crofton had finished clearing the driveway and was nowhere in sight now.

Jodie walked toward the end of the lawn, with no particular plan in mind, scuffing her feet through the soft, new-fallen snow. If Peter was here, she could help him make a snowman, she thought. But it wasn't much fun to make a snowman all alone.

She scooped up a handful of snow and molded a snowball. It was good for packing, perfect for snowballs, snow forts, and snowmen. She threw the snowball at the trunk of a big oak tree at the end of the driveway. As it splattered against the rough bark of the tree a voice shouted out, "Good shot!"

Jodie turned around with surprise and saw a boy and a collie dog coming toward her from the patch of woods at the edge of Aunt Winifred's lawn.

The dog was brown and white, with a silky coat and a graceful, slender head. The boy was taller than Jodie. He had a cheerful face, dark curly hair, and dark eyes. He was wearing a blue down jacket, corduroy pants tucked into the tops of high boots, and a red wool cap pulled down close around his head. His face was bright with cold, and he looked like he had been outside a while.

"Hi," the boy said, as he came closer. He scooped up some snow and aimed at the same tree. His snowball hit just above the white mark Jodie's snowball had left on the tree trunk.

Jodie jammed her hands in her coat pockets and eyed the boy.

"I'm Kenny Neal," the boy said. "I live down the road." He gestured back toward the woods. His dog frisked around, sweeping the snow with its plumy tail.

"Hi." Jodie's hands dragged down on the pockets. She was squinting because of the brightness of the snow all around.

"Are you visiting Mrs. Sutton?"

Jodie nodded.

The boy waited for her to say something more.

"She's my aunt," Jodie paused, then added, "my great-aunt."

Kenny scooped up more snow and aimed at the tree again, hitting almost the same spot.

"Your turn." He pushed back his cap and grinned at Jodie.

Of course, now that someone was watching, she couldn't hit anything. She couldn't hit the tree, and if a house had been there she couldn't have hit *that* either. Her snowball sailed past the tree and landed in the middle of a bush by the roadway.

"Okay!" Kenny had his next snowball ready, and aimed it right after Jodie's, past the oak tree to the bush by the road.

Jodie wanted to laugh. She felt easier now, and scooped up more snow. They began throwing fast and furious at anything and everything — tree trunks, bushes, the ornamental posts marking the entrance to the driveway — while the collie ran back and forth barking with joy.

When they finally ran out of targets, Jodie leaned against one of the driveway posts to get her breath. Kenny leaned against the trunk of the big oak tree.

"Were you just out walking in the woods?" Jodie asked, looking at Kenny across the short patch of snow between them. He was older than she was, taller and stronger. She began to feel shy again, and looked away.

"Cap likes to run in the woods," Kenny said. "He likes snow. Some dogs don't, you know."

Jodie looked at the beautiful collie that stood quietly by Kenny's side, resting from all the excitement of the snowball game.

"His name's Captain, but we just call him Cap most of the time."

"That's a nice name," Jodie said politely.

"Yeah, well — " Kenny shrugged and didn't seem to know what to say next.

Maybe he's shy, too, Jodie thought. She looked at a spot of sky just over Kenny's left shoulder and tried to think of something else to say.

"Hey — you never told me your name," Kenny said.

"It's Jodie. Jodie Linville."

"How come I haven't seen you around here before?"

"I haven't been here for a while," Jodie answered vaguely.

Kenny wanted to know where she lived, so Jodie told him about coming from Whittier on the train.

"My cousin is here, too," she said. "And my Aunt Claire. It's sort of a family reunion."

"Didn't your folks come?"

Jodie looked toward the woods across the road. She put her hands in her pockets again. Her gloves were wet with snow and her fingers were cold.

"Well, no, my mother couldn't come this time," she said.

She looked down at the ground and rubbed the toe of her boot back and forth, making a track through the snow.

"And my father's dead."

Kenny was silent for a moment. Then he said, "Gee, that's too bad. . . . Linville? I remember something about that name — "

"He died near here," Jodie said. "He was driving with my Uncle Phillip. It was snowy and their car went off the road. You probably heard about it, if you live around here."

"Sure, I remember that accident." But Kenny was thinking of more than the car accident. "Wasn't there something about some money — that rich

43

guy in town, what's-his-name — Carring, Carrington, something like that. He had a lot of money stolen."

"Fifty thousand dollars," Jodie said.

"That's a lot of money, all right," Kenny agreed. "Then his attorney died, and after the car accident they never found the money." Kenny was looking at Jodie with surprise. "Was that your dad, *that* Mr. Linville?"

"He never took any money!" Jodie said with a flush of anger. How dare this boy even think that! She wished he would go away, but he just stood there, looking at her. Jodie turned and ran back toward the house, feeling cross and unhappy.

"Hey, wait — I didn't mean anything." Kenny caught up with her, but Jodie kept on running and he let her go. "I'm really sorry — " she heard him call after her, but didn't look back. She just wanted to get inside the house, away from him.

She was almost to the front door, when it swung open and Lisa came out. Jodie had to cover up her feelings fast. She certainly didn't want Lisa to see how mad she was and ask why. Probably Lisa thought Daddy stole the money, too!

"Who's your friend?" Lisa asked, rolling her eyes toward Kenny. Jodie looked back over her shoulder, but Kenny was already walking away. Cap was frisking at his heels, as the two of them started into the woods.

"Kenny something," Jodie mumbled. She kept her face turned away from Lisa, and tried to act as if nothing had happened. They watched until Kenny and Cap were out of sight.

"He's cute," Lisa said. "What were you talking about?"

"Nothing," Jodie said. "We were just throwing snowballs."

Now that the cute boy was gone, Lisa lost interest in being outside. "It's too cold out here," she said, and went back into the house. Aunt Claire came scooting out of the living room the moment she heard Lisa and Jodie come in.

"I thought you were practicing," she told Lisa crossly. "I came downstairs and you were gone."

"Oh, Mother." Lisa darted a glance toward Jodie, who looked away. It was embarrassing to have Lisa scolded right in front of her.

Aunt Claire frowned and glanced at Jodie, too. She felt as big as an elephant, or at least as much in the way as an elephant would be.

"Well, it *is* Christmas." Aunt Claire's tone changed. She fiddled with her beads and smiled without really smiling. Jodie knew she was still cross inside.

Jodie felt very much in the way. "I think I'll go upstairs and hang these gloves somewhere to dry," she said quickly. "They're a mess."

She pulled off the soggy gloves and Aunt Claire's

45

eyebrows lifted, as though to say anyone should know better than to make snowballs. Naturally the gloves were a mess.

"Lisa — " Aunt Claire moved her head an inch toward the living room. Jodie knew this meant: "Follow me into the living room."

Lisa sighed and made a face, but she followed her mother into the living room.

Jodie could hear Aunt Claire's voice, and she went up the stairs. She went so slowly she was hardly moving at all.

"It may be the Christmas holidays, Lisa," Aunt Claire said. Her voice was low and urgent, but it could be heard in the silence of the hallway. "How interested do you think Aunt Winifred is going to be in helping with your career if she never hears you practicing?"

"But I did practice — I practiced an hour — " Lisa tried to say, but Aunt Claire rushed on without listening.

"I've explained to Aunt Winifred that you should go abroad to study, to Europe. Think of it, Lisa, *Europe*. Don't you want that? Do you want to be stuck in some dreary little town all of your life?"

There was silence in the living room.

". . . no," Lisa answered at last. "But, Mother — "

"Aunt Winifred isn't going to give you money to study music in Europe if she never hears you practicing, is she?"

"I don't know — I guess not."

Jodie was going so slowly now, she wasn't even moving. She knew she should feel guilty about eavesdropping, but she didn't — at least not very much.

Lisa was going to Europe to study music — how exciting! Jodie thought about the will. Aunt Winifred would leave Lisa a lot of money, because she was talented and needed to study abroad.

Suddenly Jodie realized how terrible it would be if Aunt Claire and Lisa came out of the living room and saw her standing on the stairs. She began to run up the stairway, clutching her wet gloves. Whatever else Aunt Claire said to Lisa was left behind.

Seven

All afternoon Lisa practiced the piano. At least it seemed like all afternoon to Jodie, who helped Mrs. Crofton make apple tarts for dinner. She rolled out the crust with the big rolling pin, and put it into the round tart pans. The kitchen was warm and cozy.

Mrs. Crofton pared the apples. She could pare an apple so the peeling came off in one long spiral. "It just takes practice," she said.

Jodie watched Mrs. Crofton's plump fingers and the curling red strip of apple peeling. Then she looked up at Mrs. Crofton's face, and Mrs. Crofton smiled. Jodie thought how much she would miss Mrs. Crofton when . . . it was sad to think of changes.

"Where will you go when Aunt Winifred dies?" Jodie asked softly. Mrs. Crofton's smile wavered for a moment, and then came back. "Why, darlin', Crofton and I have money saved up and our minds set on living near Bridgeton. We've both got relatives in that area, and there's nice, pretty spots to live. Now, don't look so sad. I'll have my own garden, and Crofton will putter and fix up, and we'll be happy as larks."

"That sounds nice," Jodie said. But she would never see Mrs. Crofton anymore when she went to live in this new place.

"Not that we won't miss your Aunt Winifred and this lovely house," Mrs. Crofton added. "We've had happy years here we'll never forget."

"What will happen to the house, do you suppose?" Jodie could hardly bear to ask.

"It will be sold, I expect," Mrs. Crofton answered slowly. The apples were all pared, and she began to cut them into slices for the tart filling. "The house will be part of the estate — but come now, that's a ways off yet — let's not be rushing on ahead of ourselves. We've got plenty to keep our minds on today — these tarts here for one thing, isn't that so?"

"That's so," Jodie said, smiling back at Mrs. Crofton.

Aunt Winifred was resting in her room, as she did now in the afternoons. When she came downstairs, it was after four o'clock. The daylight was already fading. December days were short. By four-thirty it was nearly dark.

Lisa and Jodie were picking up Christmas tree

needles that had fallen on the carpet around the tree. Aunt Claire was upstairs changing for dinner. She had so many beautiful clothes — Jodie hadn't seen her in the same outfit twice.

Aunt Winifred settled into her favorite chair by the fireplace. Crofton had made a wonderful fire for them and the flames leaped brightly on the stone hearth.

"Why don't you telephone your mother," Aunt Winifred suggested to Jodie. "Now that things are quiet," she added, winking slyly. Lisa had *finally* stopped practicing.

There was a phone in the living room, and for Aunt Winifred's convenience, it was on the table beside her favorite chair. She folded her small, fragile hands in her lap and watched Jodie dialing. Jodie had phoned the night before, to let her mother know she had arrived safely, but Peter had been in bed. This time Peter answered the phone himself, and Jodie could hear him calling their mother.

"Are you playing with your Christmas toys?" Jodie asked.

"I'm playing with my spaceship," Peter said.

It was good to hear his voice coming so clearly from so many miles away. She knew he would be kneeling on the chair by the telephone. When Mama came to take her turn to talk to Jodie, Peter would scramble down and stand by the chair listening to what Mama said.

After Jodie talked to her mother a few minutes, Aunt Winifred signaled that she wanted the phone. Jodie listened while Aunt Winifred told Mama how happy she was to have Jodie visiting her.

"I'm afraid there isn't enough for these young ladies to do," Aunt Winifred said, forgetting that Lisa had plenty to do at the piano. "They used to play in the attic when they were little, but I guess they're too grown-up for that now."

Jodie remembered those times well: warm summer afternoons playing "dress-up" with clothes from the attic trunks, the windows pushed open to let in the afternoon breeze. Winter afternoons when the attic was chilly and they had to put on extra sweaters. They played with all the wonderful old toys Aunt Winifred had kept for years and years — since Jodie's and Lisa's fathers had been little boys and played in her attic themselves.

As soon as Aunt Winifred hung up the phone Jodie said, "Remember when we used to play in the attic, Lisa?"

"That dusty old place." Lisa wrinkled her nose.

"It was *not*," Jodie protested. But Aunt Winifred smiled and said, "There was probably a speck or two of dust. Your fathers didn't mind though. They loved to play in the attic."

There was affection in her voice as she thought back over the years. "Such dear boys they were," she said wistfully.

Jodie thought maybe Aunt Winifred was going to cry, but after a moment she smiled again and said, "They played in the attic for hours and hours sometimes. I think that's why they liked to visit me. I was very popular because of my attic."

Lisa giggled, and even Jodie laughed. But it made her sad to think about her father playing in the attic when he was a little boy . . . long ago.

The room was quiet as the cousins watched their aunt nodding to herself, remembering other years. Then Lisa broke the silence.

"I have to practice some more," she said importantly.

Jodie thought Aunt Winifred looked rather sorry to hear this, as Lisa had already been playing half the day and Aunt Winifred enjoyed peace and quiet.

"Aren't your fingers tired?" Jodie asked bluntly.

"No, they aren't," Lisa snapped and flounced over to the piano bench. Aunt Winifred closed her eyes and sighed to herself.

Jodie was still thinking about the attic, and the more she thought about it the more she wanted to go up and look around.

After dinner, when Aunt Winifred and Aunt Claire were talking over their coffee, and Lisa was running up Aunt Winifred's phone bill calling all her friends at home, Jodie decided to go up to the attic.

". . . you saw Bobby Hilstrom! . . . oh, that's terrific . . . does he still like Mary Ann? I don't see what he sees in her. . . ." Lisa's voice from the living room grew fainter and fainter as Jodie went up the stairs. When she reached the upstairs hall she couldn't hear Lisa at all. Everything was very quiet.

She went along the hallway, past the bedrooms, to the narrow back stairway that led up to the attic. The stairs were dimly lighted, but Jodie knew them well.

The attic door stuck for a moment. Jodie wondered if anyone came up to the attic anymore. She pulled harder and the door scraped open. It was pitch dark in the attic, except near the windows where reflected light from the snowy countryside gave a pale cast to the windowpanes.

Jodie moved her fingers along the wall by the door, found the switch, and turned on the attic light.

She had not been in the attic since the day Mama told Aunt Winifred they were going to move away from East Hill. Aunt Winifred had sent her to the attic to find something for Peter to play with. It had been a cold, gray March afternoon.

Everything looked just the same as it had on

that March afternoon. Jodie glanced around the attic, uncertain now as to why she had come. She was too old to play with the toys or dress up in the old clothes. And she was too old to play hide-and-seek in the silent, shadowy back section where old furniture stood like the empty rooms of a ghost house, casting images on the attic floor.

The attic was quite tidy, not a jumble like some others. The toy shelves were in the front section, and there was a big wooden toy box for the smaller toys. Aunt Winifred had never had any children of her own. She kept the toys for visiting children. All she asked was that the children who played in the attic put things in order when they were finished playing. The small toys were put away into the toy box, and the larger toys on the shelves by the windows.

Jodie went over to the shelves and looked at the toys she had played with when she was younger.

Beyond the attic windows moonlight streaked the snow-covered lawn below with the shadows of trees. The night-dark countryside stretched into the distance.

Jodie shivered in the chill of the attic. Why had she come? Why had she ever liked the attic? It wasn't the same now. It was lonely and cold, and she wanted to get away. She turned off the attic light and shut the door. But something nagged at the back of her mind. Something she was trying to remember . . . or something she wanted to change . . . or something she had forgotten to do . . . what?

She stopped on the stairs and looked back. The attic door was closed. The attic light was off, she knew she had remembered to turn it off. Everything in the attic was in dark shadows again. What was she trying to remember? Why did she feel there was something wrong?

Jodie stood on the stairway and stared at the closed door. She didn't want to go back into the attic. It was dark and cold there, and she didn't know what she would be going back to find. Maybe she could just open the door and look around for a moment. But look for what?

Jodie rubbed her hand along the railing of the stairway. Something was wrong. Something was wrong in the attic. Only she didn't know *what*.

Finally, after what seemed like a long time, she started back up the stairs. She opened the attic door and switched the light on again. Everything was just the same. The old furniture, shadowy in the back section. The toy box and the shelves by the windows with everything neatly in place.

Jodie walked toward the shelves slowly. Nothing seemed wrong. She stood for a few moments, listening to the silence of the attic. At last she walked closer to the shelves. If the house was going to be sold someday, what would happen to the toys? Maybe they would be thrown away, or sold with the house. She wanted to choose a toy for a remembrance, a keepsake; Aunt Winifred wouldn't mind, she was sure. The log cabin, maybe — that had been Daddy's favorite toy. He told Jodie when he was a small boy and had played in the attic, that it was the log cabin he liked best.

There were six small Indians made of lead with the cabin, and pioneer people two inches high who lived in it. There were cows, horses, and pigs, and a cat and a dog. All of them were made of lead. You could hold a whole barnyard of animals in your open hands.

Jodie smiled to herself, remembering. She had played with the log cabin, too, sometimes. And she knew right where it was. Its put-away place was always at the end of the lower shelf.

She looked down toward the corner, but now an old spinning-top was the last thing on the shelf. It didn't fill the space the log cabin had filled. But there it lay, on its side, the bright-colored painted rings scratched and faded with age.

Jodie touched the top and it rolled lopsidedly away from her. She looked all along the lower shelf, and then all along the upper shelf — past the old-fashioned red, tin fire engine, the tiny tea set, old dolls in dusty dresses, the box of building blocks, and the stuffed animals.

But the log cabin was gone. Daddy's favorite

toy. Jodie hugged her arms to keep warm. The attic wasn't fun anymore. It was dark and gloomy and cold. There was nothing she wanted there any longer, nothing she wanted to look at anymore.

She turned off the light and closed the attic door. She went down the stairs and this time she didn't even stop to look back. In her mind's eye she could see the attic behind her, dark and cold, with the snowy landscape stretching out below the windows, and the bare trees standing in the winter woods.

Eight

The sun was bright on the snow the next morning as Jodie and Lisa sat together at one end of the long dining room table. Plates of spicy brown sausages, scrambled eggs, and toast were set out on the table.

Aunt Winifred always had her breakfast in bed. Mrs. Crofton was preparing her tray, when Aunt Claire brought the news that Aunt Winifred was not feeling well.

"Maybe just some tea and toast," Jodie heard Aunt Claire tell Mrs. Crofton in the kitchen.

"The egg is already boiled," Mrs. Crofton said, and Aunt Claire replied, "Oh, very well. Put it on the tray then."

Aunt Claire came back through the dining room, carrying the breakfast tray for Aunt Winifred.

"I'll take it up." Jodie put down her fork and started to push back her chair. But Aunt Claire shook her head.

"You're still eating," she said quickly. "Lisa can take it."

Lisa was still eating, too, but she pushed the last of her toast into her mouth, wiped her fingers on her napkin, and got up to take the tray.

Jodie could see Aunt Winifred's breakfast, neatly arranged on the tray. A soft boiled egg in a blue china egg cup. A flat dish with a silver cover that was probably toast. A small glass bowl with strawberry jam, and a teapot and teacup.

It was a full tray, but Jodie could have carried it easily. She watched as Aunt Claire handed the tray carefully to Lisa. "Mind the teapot," Aunt Claire cautioned.

"I'll help." Jodie started to get up again, but Aunt Claire waved her back down.

"We can't all be up there bothering Auntie," Aunt Claire said.

Jodie felt left out. Lisa carried the tray carefully across the hallway to the stairs.

Aunt Claire went back to the kitchen to get the pot of coffee Mrs. Crofton always made for her. Coffee was her only breakfast. She sat down across the table from Jodie and began to make her plans for the day.

"I think I'll drive into town and do a little shopping," she mused, turning her head to look outside. The sky was a cloudless blue, so there would be no more snow falling for a while.

Jodie tried to look invisible, so Aunt Claire wouldn't notice her and say, "You can come into town with me, if you like." In town Jodie might meet people like Kenny Neal, people who remembered Charles Linville and Mr. Carrington's money. She didn't want people staring at her and whispering behind her back. What if someone came right up to her and said, "Aren't you the girl whose father stole all that money?"

No, Jodie didn't want to go into town, but she wished Aunt Claire would go. As soon as she went, Jodie was going straight up to Aunt Winifred's room. Just for a minute, just to say, "Hi." She wasn't going to "bother Auntie." Maybe when lunch time came she could carry up the tray if Aunt Winifred was still in her room — and if Aunt Claire was away in town.

"On the other hand, perhaps I shouldn't leave when Auntie isn't feeling well," Aunt Claire said. She tried to sound concerned, but there was annoyance in her voice. She wanted Winifred to be well, and up and out of bed, so she wouldn't feel guilty about going into town.

"We'll be here," Jodie said. She didn't want Aunt Claire to change her mind. "Lisa and me. And there's Mrs. Crofton and Crofton." It seemed to Jodie there were plenty of people to take care of Aunt Winifred if she wanted anything.

Aunt Claire sipped her coffee and looked at Jodie slyly over the rim of her cup. "If your mother were here . . . well, I think she might have had the courtesy to come and not leave all the responsibility to me. Besides, your mother knows Auntie can't live forever. It was very rude of her not to share a little of her time and make the effort to come when she was invited."

Jodie was so mad she didn't know what to say. Where was all the courage she thought she would have?

"Now, now — don't look so startled." Aunt Claire set her cup down and smiled unpleasantly. "I'm only speaking the truth. I know perfectly well why your mother is behaving so — "

Jodie's courage returned in a rush. She didn't even let Aunt Claire finish her sentence. "My mother didn't come because she didn't want to see *you*!"

Now it was Aunt Claire's turn to look startled. She stared at Jodie's flushed face for a moment. "Tsk, tsk, aren't we getting a bit dramatic?" she finally said.

"And don't say anything about my father either!" Jodie wasn't ready to stop yet. She clenched her fists in her lap and glared at her aunt. She could feel her heart beating fast, and a satisfying plan was forming in her mind. She would go right upstairs and tell Aunt Winifred good-bye. Crofton could drive her to the train and she would go home. Maybe she would never ever have to see mean Aunt Claire again in all her life.

"I haven't said one word about your father," Aunt Claire said haughtily. "Although I certainly could say quite a lot if I wanted to."

Jodie wanted to rush out of the dining room. But she wanted even more to surprise Aunt Claire. She would wait until Claire was in town shopping. Then when she came home, Jodie would be waiting with her suitcase packed, ready to go. Wouldn't Aunt Claire be surprised then! Aunt Winifred would be sorry Jodie was leaving, and would blame Aunt Claire. Lisa would be alone again without anyone her own age. It would serve them right.

"Your father," Aunt Claire began, and then she gave an impatient shake of her head. "What's the use — no one will listen to me."

She looked at Jodie, but Jodie just sat and glared and tightened her fists in her lap. Just go to town, she begged silently. Just go away and leave me alone.

Aunt Claire was not to be bullied. She finished her coffee slowly and deliberately, without giving Jodie another glance, as though she wasn't even in the room anymore.

When Mrs. Crofton came to clear the dishes, Aunt Claire told her she would be going into town. "I'll tell Crofton," Mrs. Crofton said, and went back to the kitchen with the dishes.

Aunt Claire got up without even looking at Jodie and went out of the dining room.

Gradually Jodie unclenched her hands and her heart began to slow down to normal. As soon as Aunt Claire left the house, she was going right up to Aunt Winifred's room. She wished Aunt Claire would hurry up and go. But of course, she didn't go right away. She spent a long time getting ready, dressing herself in a white wool dress and jade jewelry. She came downstairs at last, adjusting the clasp of a bracelet, scenting the air with her expensive perfume.

The grandfather clock in the upper hall was just striking eleven when Jodie knocked at Aunt Winifred's bedroom door. She had waited until the car, with Crofton driving and Aunt Claire wrapped in her fur coat in the backseat, had disappeared from sight through the woods on the road to town. Lisa was at the piano, sending trills and scales and finger exercises echoing through the house. Jodie was on her own.

"Come in."

Jodie barely heard Aunt Winifred's voice behind the closed bedroom door. She turned the knob and peeked in. Aunt Winifred lay propped on several large pillows with wide, ruffled borders. The shades at the windows were partly drawn to keep out the light, which was quite dazzling today on the deep snow surrounding the house in every direction.

The breakfast tray had been taken away, probably by Mrs. Crofton. Aunt Claire and Lisa had, no doubt, forgotten all about it once Lisa had delivered it and let Aunt Winifred see what a good grand-niece she was. Taking away the tray wasn't as important to them as arriving with it.

"Jodie — how nice." Aunt Winifred smiled from the nest of pillows and lifted her hand, beckoning Jodie to come to her.

Jodie always liked to be in Aunt Winifred's room. There was a clock in a big glass bell and you could see all the parts working. The clock chimed with a musical sound Jodie loved to hear. There were African violets in the north windows, and a blue sofa covered with soft pillows. Everything in Aunt Winifred's room was beautiful.

Aunt Winifred smiled up at Jodie, her face against the pillows as white as the white cloth of the ruffled cases. But her blue eyes were clear and beautiful. They made Jodie think that someone much younger and stronger was looking out through those blue eyes.

"Sit down, dear." Aunt Winifred nodded toward the bedside chair. Jodie sat down on the edge of it, leaning close to the bed so that Aunt Winifred wouldn't have to strain her voice to speak to her.

Now that Jodie was actually here in Aunt Winifred's room, it wasn't as easy to say, "I'm going home," as she had thought it would be. The anger

64

that had raged inside her against Aunt Claire had cooled. Jodie wasn't sure how to begin.

"Aunt Claire went into town."

Aunt Winifred nodded. "I know. She came to tell me, to see if she could bring me anything . . . very thoughtful." Her voice drifted away and Jodie leaned closer, a little alarmed. Aunt Winifred had closed her eyes and when she did, the pretty blue eyes were gone, and her face was very still and old and white.

Jodie was silent, and after a moment Aunt Winifred opened her eyes and smiled. Then Jodie felt better.

"And Lisa's practicing," Jodie said.

Aunt Winifred's smile deepened. "So I hear. Da-da-da-da." She ticked her head back and forth feebly, imitating a metronome keeping time with piano scales.

Jodie wondered if Aunt Winifred had been told yet that Lisa had to go study in Europe where the good schools were.

"It's so nice to have you girls here." Aunt Winifred patted Jodie's hand, which lay on the edge of the coverlet beside her. "I just wish your mother had come, and little Peter. He's growing up so fast, and I'm not seeing him."

Her voice sounded so mournful that Jodie didn't know what to say. She wanted to say that Mama had wanted to come, but she knew Aunt Winifred wouldn't believe that. Aunt Winifred knew that Mama had been terribly hurt by the talk about Daddy stealing the money. There was no point to opening up old wounds, Mama had said. When she said that, Jodie always imagined she had a cut or a burn that was healing and somebody poked it or scratched at it. Her skin felt funny when Mama said, "No point in opening up old wounds."

Aunt Winifred closed her eyes again. She kept them closed even when she started to speak again.

"Yes, I wish your mother and Peter had come with you. That would have been so nice."

"Maybe Mama will come to visit some other time," Jodie said.

As soon as she said it she thought what a good idea it was. Sometime when Aunt Claire and Lisa were not visiting, Mama, Peter, and Jodie could come. They would all come on the train together. Peter would love the train ride. Everything would be all right then.

Aunt Winifred nodded and patted Jodie's hand again. "That's a fine idea, dear," she said, "and at least you're here now."

They were both quiet then, each thinking her own thoughts. From the room below, the piano music sounded faintly, soft and far away, really very pretty. The scales and finger exercises were over. Lisa hurried past these when her mother wasn't around to hear. Now she was playing a piano piece, and it made a pleasant background music for the peaceful room where Jodie sat beside Aunt Winifred's bed.

She knew she couldn't tell Aunt Winifred she was going home. Not when Aunt Winifred was so sick and lonely, and so happy to have Jodie near her.

"Can I bring your lunch tray?" Jodie said after a bit. She thought it would be good to get that settled before Aunt Claire came home and interfered.

"Yes indeed," Aunt Winifred said. "You may bring my lunch tray."

The room was silent. Jodie wasn't sure whether to stay or go. The clock under the glass bell chimed sweetly to mark the quarter hour, then the room was silent once more.

Jodie could hear the piano from the living room below.

"I never thought your father took that money," Aunt Winifred said quietly. "Never. No one could ever make me believe that Charles did it. He was always such a good boy, and so was Phillip. Oh, they got into mischief sometimes." A smile touched Aunt Winifred's face for a moment. "They used to like to climb trees in the backyard, and when I'd shoo them down they didn't like it. But they were good boys, good boys. . . ."

Jodie wished Aunt Winifred would open her eyes. It was difficult talking to someone who had her eyes closed. It was hard for Jodie to understand that Aunt Winifred could be tired enough to close her eyes right in the middle of a conversation. But even if her eyes were closed, it was good to hear her say she knew Daddy hadn't stolen Mr. Carrington's money.

"I told your mother that, too," Aunt Winifred added. "I told her I knew your father wouldn't steal anyone's money."

She opened her eyes and looked up into Jodie's face. "You know who I think took that money, Jodie? That nephew of Mr. Carrington's — what was his name?" Aunt Winifred brushed the name aside with a motion of her hand. "Whatever it was — he's the one, that nephew."

"Do you think so?" Jodie leaned closer to the bed.

"Yes, I do," Aunt Winifred said firmly. "Indeed I do."

But almost at once the firmness faded. "We'll never know, I'm afraid," she said helplessly. "It's all too long ago now. We'll never really know."

Jodie thought of all her dreams about finding out who stole the money. She had believed that someday, some way, she would find out who stole the money. She didn't like to hear Aunt Winifred saying they would never know what really happened.

It's not too late, Jodie told herself with determination. It's *not* too late. She wasn't going home after all, and it wasn't too late to find out the truth.

Nine

Aunt Winifred stayed in her room during the afternoon, and the house had a quiet, subdued atmosphere.

"This is boring," Lisa complained as the time dragged by. "Can't we do something?"

Aunt Claire was lounging on the sofa by the Christmas tree, turning the pages of a magazine. She didn't offer any exciting suggestions. Jodie had wound a music box that stood on one of the side tables, and the delicate tinkly notes of *Silent Night* drifted softly through the room.

"You could go for a walk," said Mrs. Crofton, who was watering plants by the living room windows.

Lisa shrugged.

"You need some fresh air — all of you." Mrs. Crofton raised her voice so Aunt Claire could hear.

Jodie looked up from the music box. She wanted to see if Aunt Claire would jump up and hurry outside for a walk in the fresh air. But just the way she bent her head over the pages of the magazine showed how important it was to her, how much attention she was giving it. No one should bother her while she was reading this magazine.

"Fresh air puts roses in your cheeks," the housekeeper said to Lisa.

Jodie put the music box down carefully. The notes of *Silent Night* were fading away, faintly, slower and slower. Soon they would stop.

"I don't know." Lisa didn't sound very interested in going for a walk.

Then to Jodie's surprise she changed her mind.

"On second thought, that's not a bad idea," she said. "Come on, Jodie, let's go for a walk."

Aunt Claire lifted her head with a bemused expression, as if she was just now realizing there were other people in the room with her. "Yes, go for a walk, darling, good exercise." Then she went back to her magazine.

"You ought to get some exercise, too," Mrs. Crofton mumbled, but Aunt Claire pretended not to hear.

Jodie and Lisa put on their boots and coats and caps. Jodie wondered what made Lisa change her mind so suddenly. She didn't have to wait long to find out. They were barely down the front steps, feeling the exhilaration of the cold air after the warm rooms of the house, when Lisa said, "We ought to have some place to walk to . . . I wonder how far away that boy lives."

She said it very casually, as though she just now thought of it. Jodie's heart sank. She didn't want to see Kenny Neal again.

"He must live nearby," Lisa chattered on. "Let's see if we can find his house."

"I don't think we can find it," Jodie argued, as she followed Lisa toward the road. "It could be anywhere." She gestured with her arms to include all East Hill.

"Don't be silly." Lisa tossed her head. "It ought to be easy to find. It will probably be the first house we come to."

Jodie was afraid that might be true. Houses were few and far between on Old North Road. Or "far and few between" as Mama used to joke. It came to the same thing.

"Wait, you're going the wrong way," she said in desperation. Lisa stopped and looked at Jodie with surprise. "This is the way he was going," she reminded Jodie.

"He wasn't going home," Jodie said quickly. "I think he lives that way." She pointed in the very opposite direction.

Lisa didn't look convinced. "Are you sure?"

"I'm pretty sure," Jodie said. It wasn't a very

big fib, and it was better than going in the right direction and actually finding Kenny's house and maybe Kenny himself.

The first house they came to was set back from the road, almost lost from sight in the snowy landscape. No one was living there. All the shutters were closed over the windows and there was a *For Sale* sign by the driveway.

"This isn't it," Lisa said with disappointment.

They walked on, trudging by the side of the road, well out of the way of occasional passing cars.

The sky was dull blue in the distance above them, and only little by little did Jodie realize how cold she was getting. It was a long walk to the next house. When they reached it, there was a roadside mailbox with the name *Miller* printed on it. They knew that it wasn't Kenny Neal's house.

"Are you sure we're going in the right direction?" Lisa frowned at Jodie as they started on.

"It'll probably be the very next house," Jodie said. Then, to keep Lisa cheerful, she asked, "Are you really going to Europe to study music?"

To her surprise, Lisa made a face. "I hope not!" she said emphatically. "I don't want to leave my friends. My mother is the one who wants to go to Europe. I'm her big chance."

Jodie was a little surprised. Lisa looked more

annoyed than ever now, not finding Kenny's house and then being reminded she might have to go to Europe to study music.

They walked along in silence for a few minutes. Jodie shivered a little. It was getting colder. One more house and then she was going to suggest that they start back. It was going to be a long walk.

The wind was growing stronger, and Jodie could feel her eyes watering with the cold. She looked sideways at Lisa. Her face was pinched-up with cold and she didn't look very happy.

"Maybe we should turn back," Jodie said finally. "My fingers are frozen, my feet, too."

Lisa didn't need to be asked twice. "This was sure some dumb idea," she said as they started back. They both began to laugh a little then, because they were so cold and tired of walking.

"Boys!" Lisa said.

"Boys!" Jodie echoed.

It wasn't so bad being cold and tired if they could laugh together. Still, it seemed to take forever before they got back to the houses they had passed earlier.

"There's the Miller mail box!" Jodie saw it first. It was a long way yet to the closed-up house, but then they would soon be to Aunt Winifred's. Jodie still felt guilty, but at least she hadn't had to see Kenny Neal again.

Aunt Winifred's house appeared ahead at last. Late afternoon light glazed the windows with silvery reflections.

As Jodie and Lisa drew closer they could see lights in the windows on the lower floor. They could see the Christmas tree lights. Aunt Claire was probably sitting by a warm, cozy fire in the living room.

Jodie looked up toward Aunt Winifred's bedroom windows. The curtains were not completely closed and a light was shining there, too.

But on the very top floor, the windows of the attic were dark.

Ten

Aunt Winifred was eating alone in her room that evening as Jodie, Lisa, and Aunt Claire took their places at the dining room table for dinner.

The room had a warm, spicy smell. Mrs. Crofton had baked mince pies that afternoon, and the aroma still drifted through the house.

"When I was in town this morning I overheard someone saying that this has been the snowiest winter in this area for a long time," Aunt Claire remarked. Her gold earrings sparkled in the candlelight. "I suppose they've been reading *The Farmer's Almanac*," she added with amusement.

Jodie wasn't really listening. She missed Aunt Winifred. It was so much easier when Aunt Winifred was with them. She always had stories to tell. Jodie liked to hear the stories Aunt Winifred remembered from the time she was a little girl. They were always interesting and sometimes, very funny. Her brother Benjamin was always getting into trouble. He got sent to his room, and sent to the woodshed, and sent home from school. Aunt Winifred never ran out of stories about Benjamin. But Aunt Winifred was not there to tell any funny stories tonight.

Aunt Claire was describing a fat lady she had seen in town that morning, "who didn't have the sense to wear plain dark colors to make herself look thinner."

Jodie buttered a dinner roll and took a bite so she didn't have to answer. New Year's Eve was only three nights away. Jodie hoped Aunt Winifred would be feeling well enough to come downstairs and celebrate with them. Jodie didn't think New Year's Eve would be much fun with Aunt Claire.

Everyone ate in silence for a few minutes. Then just to get another conversation going, Jodie said, "I went up to the attic yesterday."

Aunt Claire and Lisa didn't seem to consider that much of an announcement.

Lisa puckered her nose. "That dusty place."

"It is not dus — " Jodie started to protest, and then stopped. What was the use. And what if the attic was a little dusty? People didn't go into attics to get clean.

"Do you remember the log cabin?" she asked Lisa. "With the little Indians and pioneers?"

"I think so." Lisa wasn't very interested.

"I couldn't find it. It was always on the bottom shelf, but it wasn't there. It wasn't anywhere."

"You probably didn't look hard enough," Lisa said matter-of-factly. Her expression said a lost toy in the attic was no big deal anyway.

"I did," Jodie said stubbornly. "I thought it ought to be there. It was my father's favorite toy."

"It was probably thrown away long ago." Aunt Claire was impatient to settle the discussion. "Auntie can't keep everything forever."

Jodie was taken aback. "But Aunt Winifred wouldn't just throw it away, would she? Daddy's favorite toy?" Jodie didn't see how even Aunt Claire could think that Aunt Winifred would do something like that.

"Maybe Auntie didn't know it was your father's favorite toy," she said, gesturing with her hands so that the bracelets on her arm jingled together.

Her tone of voice indicated she was finished talking about the toy cabin and they continued to eat their dessert in silence. The mince pie was still warm. Mrs. Crofton had topped it with whipped cream, and it was just about the best thing Jodie had ever eaten. But she was still thinking about the log cabin.

She was thinking about her yarn doll . . . I could never throw that away, Mama had said. It was your favorite toy when you were little.

Aunt Winifred had never had any children of

her own, and Charles and Phillip Linville were as dear to her as if they had been her own two little boys. Jodie had heard that often enough from Aunt Winifred, and from Daddy when he had been alive. Daddy had loved Aunt Winifred very much, and she had loved him and Uncle Phillip. Would she throw away — or give away — Daddy's log cabin, and keep so many other toys that weren't nearly as important?

Jodie wanted to go upstairs after dinner and ask Aunt Winifred what had happened to the log cabin. But of course she wouldn't tell Aunt Claire that. "We can't always be bothering Auntie," she would say. Or, "Auntie's resting, we mustn't bother her tonight."

Jodie finished her dessert. She didn't say any more about the log cabin. After dinner, she watched television with Lisa and Aunt Claire. She kept looking for a chance to slip away and go up to Aunt Winifred's room — without Aunt Claire knowing. But no chance came.

And then at last, at bedtime, Jodie had her chance. Lisa was taking a bath and Aunt Claire was still down in the living room. She would read for a while, and come to bed later. It was the perfect time to see Aunt Winifred.

Jodie was already in her pajamas, and she slipped on her new Christmas robe. She opened the door of her room and looked up and down the hall. No one was in sight. She hurried to Aunt Winifred's door and knocked as softly as she could.

If Aunt Winifred was sleeping she wouldn't even hear such a soft knock, so no harm would be done. Jodie would go away.

But almost at once Jodie heard Aunt Winifred say, "Come in," just as she had done before.

Jodie opened Aunt Winifred's door and peeked in. Aunt Winifred was lying against the ruffled pillows, just as she had been before.

The room looked different at night. The heavy blue silk drapes were drawn across the windows, and most of the room was lost in darkness. The only light came from the small lamp on Aunt Winifred's bedside table.

"Hi." Jodie stood by the bed and studied Aunt Winifred's face. She looked as though she had been sleeping and just wakened. Her white hair was flattened on one side where she had rested her head.

"I'm so sleepy," Aunt Winifred said. "It's my medicine. It makes me so sleepy."

"That's all right," Jodie said quickly. "I just came to say good-night."

"That was sweet of you." Aunt Winifred's voice was fading away and she had closed her eyes again.

"Aunt Winifred?"

The blue eyes fluttered open.

Jodie leaned close to the bed. "Aunt Winifred — did you throw away the log cabin?"

Aunt Winifred stared at Jodie without understanding. She didn't know what Jodie was talking about, Jodie could tell that right away.

"The log cabin that was in the attic," Jodie said.

Aunt Winifred's eyes were closing again. She was groggy from her medicine. In a moment she would be sound asleep.

"The log cabin that my daddy liked so much." Jodie wanted to shake Aunt Winifred's arm to keep her awake just a little longer. "You wouldn't throw that away, would you? It was his favorite toy."

Aunt Winifred shook her head. She looked confused. ". . . log cabin?"

"Aunt Winifred — did you give it away to someone?"

Aunt Winifred shook her head slowly. "I don't remember." Her words came slowly. "Maybe . . . cleaning out the attic. . . ."

She lifted one hand helplessly and then dropped it back on the bed covers. "I'm sorry, dear . . . I don't remember. . . ."

The blue eyes closed again. Jodie stood for a moment looking at the still face.

Maybe she would never know what had happened to the log cabin. But still, it was strange,

Jodie thought, as she drew back from Aunt Winifred's bed. It just didn't seem right that the cabin was gone and nobody knew anything about it.

Sometime that night Jodie awoke suddenly. She didn't know what had wakened her and lay in the dark listening, trying to hear if there were strange noises anywhere.

Sometimes in the summer, thunderstorms would wake her up; sometimes not. "Heavens," Mama would say the next morning. "How could you sleep through that storm?"

But it was December now, and she couldn't ever remember hearing a thunderstorm in December. What had wakened her?

Jodie strained her ears, but she couldn't hear anything. No stormy wind whistled around the corners of the house. No tree branches rattled against the windowpanes. She couldn't hear any sounds in the house. No one was stirring about. Everyone was asleep. Even the house seemed to be asleep — so silently did it lie around her, dark and motionless.

Then Jodie saw the attic in her mind, the two shelves by the attic windows. She had been dreaming about the attic, and there at the end of the bottom shelf was an old spinning-top lying on its side, glimmering in the light from the attic bulb.

Jodie lay back against the pillows and listened to the silence of the dark house. It was strange to be awake in the middle of the night. She wonderd if anyone else was awake. She thought of Aunt Winifred, drowsy from medication, sleeping in her beautiful blue room. The clock would softly chime the passing hours. But Aunt Winifred would not hear.

Aunt Claire? Asleep, too. Lisa? Asleep. No one was awake but Jodie. And she couldn't get back to sleep.

Somebody had put a top where the log cabin had been, so there wouldn't be an empty place on the shelf.

Why would anyone do that? Jodie pulled the cover close up around her chin and stared into the darkness.

Eleven

The next day Aunt Winifred was feeling better. She came down to sit in the living room shortly after lunch.

Aunt Claire and Lisa were in town shopping for the day. Jodie was in the kitchen helping Mrs. Crofton make tapioca pudding for Aunt Winifred's dinner when there was a knock at the back door.

"Now who's that?" Mrs. Crofton wanted to know. She and Jodie looked at each other across the counter top.

"I'll see." Jodie put down the cup she had been using to measure sugar, and went to the door. It was Kenny Neal.

Jodie was so surprised her mouth dropped open, then she got embarrassed and closed it again as quickly as she could. Behind Kenny she could see Captain chasing a squirrel across the back lawn.

"Hi." Kenny had Cap's rubber ball in his hand, worn-out and chewed-looking. He tossed it up like a juggler and caught it with his other hand. "Want to come out awhile?"

Jodie felt embarrassed. She looked over her shoulder at Mrs. Crofton.

"Hello there, Kenny." Mrs. Crofton knew everybody who lived nearby. She motioned for Kenny to come inside. "Warm up while Jodie gets ready," she said.

Kenny shook his head and pointed to his snowy boots. "I'd better wait outside."

Captain came barking toward the door and Kenny threw the rubber ball far across the lawn. Cap ran off, scattering snow around him as he ran.

Jodie went into the living room and told Aunt Winifred she was going outside for a while.

"I'll look for you," Aunt Winifred promised. She was sitting in a chair by the windows, and had a good view of the front lawn.

It didn't take Jodie long to get into her outdoor things. Kenny was running with Cap along the row of poplar trees at the end of the back lawn. They ran to meet Jodie as she came down the back steps.

"My cousin went into town," Jodie said. She wanted Kenny to know that Lisa wasn't going to come hurrying out to join them, all golden-haired and pretty.

"I came to see you," he said.

Jodie felt her face flushing. She hoped Kenny

would think it was only because of the cold.

"I wanted to apologize for the other day. I didn't mean to say anything bad about your father."

He looked so worried that Jodie couldn't stay mad at him. "Friends?" he asked, and Jodie nodded. "Friends," she said. Kenny's face brightened at once.

He leaned against the railing at the foot of the steps. "So what have you been doing since I saw you?"

"My aunt's been sick," she said. She watched as Cap frisked away after another squirrel. "She's better now. Let's go around to the front of the house. She's sitting in the living room."

Kenny whistled to Cap and they all ran along the side of the house to the big front lawn.

"There she is," Jodie said, waving her arms toward the front windows like she was hailing ships at sea.

Aunt Winifred smiled and waved back.

"She was watching for us," Jodie said. "I told her I was coming outside for a while — hey, why don't we build a snowman for her?"

"Sure," Kenny said. "She can watch."

Jodie cupped her hand around her mouth and called to Aunt Winifred: "We're going to make a snowman."

Aunt Winifred smiled and waved again.

"I don't think she heard you," Kenny said. "Come

on, we'll show her what we're going to do."

They began to roll the first big ball of snow. "This is perfect snow for a snowman," Kenny said.

Jodie heaped on more snow, until they had a ball they could roll, picking up more snow.

The snowman was soon taking shape. Aunt Winifred watched from the living room window, and Jodie saw Mrs. Crofton come to stand by Aunt Winifred's chair. Then Crofton came around the side of the house bringing two black buttons for eyes, a slice of red apple cut in a curve like a mouth, and — "The nose!" Crofton flourished a carrot.

"Very original," Kenny teased.

Jodie wished the afternoon would never end. But by and by the snowman was finished. The black button eyes were in place, and the smiling red mouth, and the long, crooked carrot nose.

Jodie looked toward the house. She was going to wave to Aunt Winifred again, but the sunlight hitting the attic windows caught her eye. The light was glistening on them, beckoning to her.

"What's the matter?" Kenny asked, as she stood staring up at the windows.

Jodie turned away quickly. "Oh, nothing," she said. She got busy scooping up more snow to pat into place on the snowman's fat stomach. She couldn't explain about the attic and the log cabin to Kenny. She couldn't blurt out, "As soon as you go home, I'm going up to the attic — I know Aunt Winifred wouldn't throw away Daddy's log cabin, it has to be there somewhere."

She couldn't say that. It would sound silly to Kenny, worrying about an old toy nobody ever played with anymore. She patted snow on the snowman.

"Hey, what's wrong?" Kenny was watching her uneasily.

"Nothing," Jodie repeated. She shook her head and pounded snow onto the fat snowman.

"You look sort of funny," Kenny said.

"I'm just cold."

Kenny hesitated. "Maybe I'll see you tomorrow," he said finally, brushing snow from his wet gloves. "Are you going to be here much longer?"

"Until after New Year's," Jodie said. She watched as Kenny and Cap went off through the woods toward Gray Road. Then she stood a few moments longer, looking at the snowman they had made.

The tilt of the carrot nose made her feel lonesome for Kenny and Cap.

Jodie went indoors, stamping her boots carefully on the mat before she walked on Mrs. Crofton's clean kitchen floor. Crofton was sitting at the table drinking coffee.

Mrs. Crofton was just coming from the front of the house, and she greeted Jodie warmly. "That's a fine-looking snowman," she said in her hearty voice. "Your aunt got a lot of pleasure watching you two make it, indeed she did."

Crofton poured himself more coffee from a pot on the table and winked at Jodie. "Fine-looking snowman," he agreed.

Jodie sat in a chair by the table and took off her boots. She put them by the back door to dry.

Unbuttoning her coat as she went, she walked along the hallway to the living room. Through the living room doorway she could see Aunt Winifred talking on the telephone. The Christmas tree lights were not lit, but a streak of sunlight coming through the window sparkled on the silvery strands of tinsel draped over the branches.

Aunt Winifred didn't see Jodie, and she went on up the stairs and along the upper hall, past the silent bedrooms where no one was sleeping now. The pendulum of the grandfather clock was moving in its steady rhythm behind the glass front. Its muted tick-tock was the only sound in the hall.

At the end of the hall a narrow flight of stairs led down to the kitchen, and another flight led up to the attic. Jodie could hear muffled noises from the kitchen — the sound of Crofton's deep voice, Mrs. Crofton's laugh.

Jodie looked up the attic steps, to the closed attic door. Then she started up.

She was going to find the log cabin this time. It wasn't on the shelf where it had always been, and she wanted to know where it was, and why it wasn't in its right place.

Twelve

Jodie stood in the attic again, alone in the glare of light from the big window. She looked carefully along each shelf to see if the log cabin had mysteriously reappeared; but it was not there.

She knelt by the toy box — why hadn't she thought of that before! Someone had probably put the log cabin away in the wrong place. The lid of the toy box was stuck and it took several strenuous tugs before Jodie could wrench it loose. The handle was a metal ring, and it dug into the palm of her hand as she struggled. But at last the lid jerked free and she lifted it to look inside the box.

There were small toys all jumbled together. Jodie pawed through them recklessly. Something as big as the log cabin would be found at once! But it was not there. Knowing it was useless, Jodie still pushed and rummaged through the toys. There were rubber balls, blocks, loose dominoes, a pack of Old Maid playing cards, a bag of jacks, paper money from some long-lost Monopoly game, and pieces of a jigsaw puzzle. But nothing big and solid and sturdy like a log cabin. Then near the bottom of the toy box Jodie saw a little lead Indian. She searched eagerly through the jumble of things in the toy box and found several more Indians, some pioneer people, cows, pigs, and a horse.

It looked as if the figures had been dumped into the box, and then everything was shuffled around so they were all separated from each other and mixed in with the odds and ends of loose toys. Why would anyone do that?

Jodie kept looking, finding more and more pieces, another pig, a cat, another Indian. She lined the Indians, the pioneer people, and the animals along the windowsill. There was even the little pioneer baby in its tiny cradle-bed.

There was still no log cabin, but Jodie felt inspired now. She dragged the old clothes trunk over to the window and lifted the lid. The lid wasn't stuck, but it was hard to lift. It was a heavy, old trunk with brass corners and a dulled brass hasp. Inside were all the dress-up clothes Jodie and Lisa had played with when they were little girls.

On top, being most fragile, were the old hats with wispy feathers and silky, fluttering ribbons. Jodie lifted them out one by one. Here was the fan she loved so much, the cane with the ivory handle, the long dress Lisa always chose and always tripped over because it was so long. "You'll break your neck," Aunt Claire said when she saw Lisa in that long dress. But Lisa had not broken even a fingernail.

Excited by her discovery in the toy box, Jodie was sure with each skirt and shawl and old hat she lifted from the clothes trunk that any moment she would uncover the log cabin, put away for whatever reason into the trunk. Perhaps to protect it, she thought. Any reason would do, if she could just find the log cabin. It was the only toy she cared about. It had been her father's favorite toy, and Jodie remembered playing with it when she was little, when climbing the stairs to Aunt Winifred's attic had been a long climb for her short legs.

Sometimes Lisa had been with her. They had built a fence of blocks around the log cabin and a pigpen with blocks. They put the cows outside the fence to graze in the meadows, and the Indians high up on the top of the toy box. The toy box was the mountain where the Indians lived. They put the pioneer people in the log cabin, and the Indians came down from the mountain and sold them beads and blankets. Those days of playing seemed long ago.

Everything was out of the trunk now. Jodie was surrounded by piles of musty, wrinkled old clothes. The bottom of the trunk was lined with ancient, yellowing sheets of tissue paper, and there were a few stray feathers that had fallen off the hats during the years.

Jodie sank back wearily. Her wonderful idea had come to nothing. The log cabin was not in the clothes trunk.

After she put all the clothes back into the trunk, she closed the lid and sat down on the trunk with a discouraged sigh. The little lead Indians, settlers, and farm animals stood motionless along the windowsill.

Jodie turned away and looked toward the back of the attic at the old furniture that had once been used downstairs in the house: a flowered sofa, grown dark and dim, several large chests of drawers, two cane chairs with saggy seats, a round oak table. Boxes marked *Christmas Ornaments* and *Christmas Lights* were in the middle of the furniture area. Usually they would have been against the back wall.

Jodie wandered over into the "ghost room" of furniture. The Christmas boxes were empty, as she had suspected. All the ornaments and lights were downstairs on the tree.

But along the back wall there were other boxes. Maybe someone had packed the log cabin away in one of them.

Most of the boxes were neatly marked with heavy black crayon. Jodie saw boxes marked *Photographs*, *Green Drapes*, *Aunt Ellen's Teapot*, and

Candles. None was marked *Toys* or *Log Cabin*. The boxes were tied with twine, firmly knotted; but Jodie didn't really want to look through them all. She began to wander aimlessly, looking into the drawers of the old chests, poking around restlessly, disappointed that she hadn't found the cabin. Most of the drawers were empty. In one, a pencil rolled across the drawer bottom as Jodie pulled the drawer open.

She peeked under the old sofa and found several old magazines. Behind one of the chests of drawers she found an umbrella leaning against the wall.

And then behind another chest of drawers, which stood well away from the wall, she found the log cabin. Just when she was about to give up, she had found the log cabin!

An old cloth had been hastily thrown over it, not covering it all.

Jodie was so surprised that she cried out with excitement as she reached down to grasp the cabin and pull it out from behind the chest. A corner of the cabin caught on an uneven floorboard, and the cabin almost tipped over. Something inside shifted, and Jodie saw the corner of a small box poke out through the cabin door.

The roof of the cabin lifted off so you could play with the pioneer family inside. When Jodie had pulled the cabin to a clear space on the attic floor, she knelt down and lifted up the roof. Inside was a large pouch made of brown suede, and it was full of money. Lots and lots of money, all one-hundred-dollar bills. On the front of the pouch was the initial *C*. Jodie traced the curve of the letter with her finger ". . . Carrington," she whispered. The box that had slid to the opening of the cabin door was small with the name of the jeweler in fancy gold lettering on the lid: REGENT JEWELERS.

Jodie's fingers were shaking as she snapped open the box. Glittering on a red velvet lining were two earrings that looked like circles of diamonds. Jodie touched them to see if she was dreaming. But she wasn't. They were real. Real diamond earrings!

A card was tucked under the earrings. Jodie lifted it up, her fingers still trembling with excitement.

> *To my dear wife Claire — a special gift*
> *for a special lady*
> *Your loving husband Phillip*

Jodie crouched silently beside the log cabin, holding the note in her hand. She felt far away from the attic, and the house, from Aunt Winifred and Mrs. Crofton, as if she were on the moon. Nothing existed but the glittering diamond earrings, and the note Uncle Phillip had written to Aunt Claire.

Voices echoed in her mind: her mother's, Aunt Winifred's, Aunt Claire's. Talk about Mr. Carrington, about Daddy, about Mr. Carrington's nephew. About money kept in a safety deposit box at the bank, the bank where Uncle Phillip was a vice-president, the money was gone, the safety deposit box was empty. We'll find out the truth, Uncle Phillip promised . . . we'll find out the truth.

And all the time it had been Uncle Phillip himself.

Jodie stared at the earrings, at the bundles of hundred-dollar bills, at the note. *To my dear wife Claire.*

Uncle Phillip had stolen the money from the safety deposit box in the bank. How did he do it? Jodie wondered. She knew Daddy had a key to the deposit box — that's why some people thought he had taken the money. Maybe Uncle Phillip had a key, too, since he was a vice-president of the bank. Or maybe he got hold of Daddy's key somehow and used it, or had a duplicate made from it. Uncle Phillip was dead so they would never know for sure how he had managed to get into the safety deposit box.

After he had stolen the money, he had hidden it in the log cabin in Aunt Winifred's attic. Nobody thought of looking for the money there! He had bought the diamond earrings to surprise Aunt Claire. But he had died before he could come back to the attic and move his stolen money to a better hiding place, or give Aunt Claire the beautiful earrings.

All this time, while everyone was trying to find out who stole the money, the money was here in the attic in the log cabin. It had been here the day Jodie came up to find something for Peter to play with. She had been so close to it, without ever knowing!

Jodie was so deep in thought, so stunned by her discovery, that she had no idea how long she had been up in the attic. She came back to reality with a peculiar light-headed feeling. Far away in the house below, she heard a telephone ringing. She stood up and carried the jewelry box to the window to see how the earrings would look in the sunlight.

But the sunlight had shifted. The toy Indians and pioneers and animals on the windowsill were now in shadow. In the driveway below, the car was returning from town with Aunt Claire and Lisa.

Jodie stared down as the car came to a stop and Crofton got out to open the door for Aunt Claire. Lisa opened the door on her side herself and stepped out into the driveway. She started walking toward the house with her mother.

Lisa isn't so bad, Jodie thought. Sometimes she was pretty nice. It wasn't her fault Aunt Claire spoiled her so much. It wouldn't be easy for her to learn that her father was a thief.

Jodie even felt sorry for Aunt Claire. She was walking beside Crofton, who was carrying all the packages she had bought in town. "She knows how to spend money," Daddy always joked. Once he had even said it to Aunt Claire: "Claire, you certainly know how to spend money."

"It's nice to do something really well," Aunt Claire had said.

It had all been in fun. Uncle Phillip had laughed along with everyone else.

It would be a shock to Aunt Claire to find out that Uncle Phillip had stolen the money. It would be a sad thing for both Lisa and Aunt Claire to find out.

They were in the house now. Jodie couldn't see anything but the car on the driveway. After a minute, Crofton came back outside and got into the car. He drove it around the side of the house toward the garage. No one was going anywhere else today. He would put the car away until tomorrow. Then he would go into the kitchen and talk to Mrs. Crofton as she worked at the counter in the kitchen.

Jodie turned away from the window at last. She put the brown pouch and the box of earrings with the card from Uncle Phillip back into the log cabin and closed the roof.

She looked once more around the attic where she had played so many times, where her father and uncle had played when they were children, played with favorite toys.

Late afternoon light slanted through the windows across the toy shelves. The small lead figures of Indians, pioneers, and animals still stood along the windowsill.

The cabin wasn't heavy, but it was awkward to carry. Jodie nudged the light switch with her elbow and pushed the attic door open with her foot. Then she started carefully down the stairs to show Aunt Winifred what she had found.

She felt sad that Daddy was dead, that Uncle Phillip — jolly Uncle Phillip — had wanted money so much he had stolen it. But another part of her was happy. Jodie knew how much her discovery would mean to Mama.

And now no one could ever again say that her father was a thief.

About the Author

Carol Beach York has written many books for children, including many juvenile mysteries for Scholastic. She lives in Chicago.

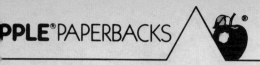

PPLE®PAPERBACKS

Mystery! Adventure! Drama! Humor!
Apple® paperbacks have it all!

NEW APPLE® TITLES! $1.95 each

☐ QI 32877-8 **Tough-Luck Karen**   Johanna Hurwitz
☐ QI 33139-6 **Bummer Summer**   Ann M. Martin
☐ QI 33271-6 **The Telltale Summer of Tina C.**   Lila Perl
☐ QI 33300-3 **Encyclopedia Brown Sets the Pace**   Donald J. Sobol
☐ QI 33103-5 **Tarantulas on the Brain**   Marilyn Singer
☐ QI 33298-8 **Amy Moves In**   Marilyn Sachs
☐ QI 33299-6 **Laura's Luck**   Marilyn Sachs
☐ QI 32299-0 **Amy and Laura**   Marilyn Sachs
☐ QI 32464-0 **Circle of Gold**   Candy Dawson Boyd
☐ QI 32522-1 **Getting Rid of Marjorie**   Betty Ren Wright

BEST-SELLING APPLE® TITLES

☐ QI 32188-9 **Nothing's Fair in Fifth Grade**   Barthe DeClements
☐ QI 32548-5 **The Secret of NIMH**™   Robert C. O'Brien
☐ QI 32157-9 **The Girl with the Silver Eyes**   Willo Davis Roberts
☐ QI 32500-0 **The Cybil War**   Betsy Byars
☐ QI 32427-6 **The Pinballs**   Betsy Byars
☐ QI 32437-3 **A Taste of Blackberries**   Doris Buchanan Smith
☐ QI 31957-4 **Yours Till Niagara Falls, Abby**   Jane O'Connor
☐ QI 32556-6 **Kid Power**   Susan Beth Pfeffer

■ Scholastic Inc.
P.O. Box 7502, 2932 E. McCarty Street, Jefferson City, MO 65102

Please send me the books I have checked above. I am enclosing $_____
please add $1.00 to cover shipping and handling). Send check or money order—no cash or
C.O.D.'s please.

Name_____

Address_____

City_____ State/Zip_____

APP851   Please allow four to six weeks for delivery.

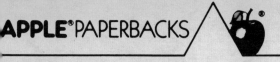

BETSY BYARS
from Apple® Paperbacks
Your favorite authors...
your favorite books!

NEW APPLE® PAPERBACKS
BY BETSY BYARS   **$1.95 each**
☐ QI 32925-1   **The Two-Thousand Pound Goldfish**

OTHER APPLE PAPERBACKS
BY BETSY BYARS   **$1.95 each**
☐ QI 32500-0   **The Cybil War**
☐ QI 32425-X   **Goodbye, Chicken Little**
☐ QI 32427-6   **The Pinballs**
☐ QI 32135-8   **Trouble River**
☐ QI 32555-8   **The TV Kid**

Scholastic Inc.
P.O. Box 7502, 2932 E. McCarty Street, Jefferson City, MO 65102

Please send me the books I have checked above. I am enclosing $ _____
(please add $1.00 to cover shipping and handling). Send check or money order—no
cash or C.O.D.'s please.

Name _____

Address _____

City_____ State/Zip _____

APP853   Please allow four to six weeks for delivery.